VOLUME 5: THE NEW PATH

OUTCAST BY KIRKMAN & AZACETA
VOL. 5: THE NEW PATH
September 2017
First printing

ISBN: 978-1-5343-0249-5

Published by Image Comics, Inc.

Office of publication: 2701 NW Vaughn St., Ste. 780,
Portland, OR 97210.

Printed in the U.S.A.

For information regarding the CPSIA on this printed material call: 203-595-3636 and provide reference # RICH - 762783.

Robert Kirkman
Creator, Writer

Paul Azaceta
Artist

Elizabeth Breitweiser
Colorist

Rus Wooton
Letterer

Paul Azaceta
Elizabeth Breitweiser
Cover

Arielle Basich
Assistant Editor

Sean Mackiewicz
Editor

Rian Hughes
Logo Design

WHERE ARE WE GOING, MOMMY?

WE'RE GOING HOME WITH YOUR DADDY, AMBER. WE'RE GOING TO STAY WITH HIM FOR A LITTLE WHILE.
REALLY?!

THAT'S RIGHT, KIDDO. YOU EXCITED?
AM I GOING TO HAVE MY OWN ROOM?

WE STILL HAVE TO FIGURE THAT OUT--THIS ALL CAME TOGETHER REALLY FAST.
IT'S GOING TO BE A FUN SLEEPOVER, DEAR--WE MIGHT EVEN ALL BE SLEEPING ON THE FLOOR TOGETHER LIKE WE'RE CAMPING.
COOL!
COUPLE MORE MINUTES. TOLD YOU WE'D MAKE IT BACK BEFORE SUNUP.

I THOUGHT WE WERE STAYING AWAY FROM DADDY BECAUSE YOU THOUGHT HE WAS BAD.
TURNS OUT I WAS WRONG. IT'S BAD TO BE AWAY FROM DADDY. SO THAT'S WHY WE'RE ALL GOING TO BE TOGETHER AGAIN.

IS THAT WHY EVERYBODY LOOKS AT ME ALL THE TIME? BECAUSE OF DADDY?

YOU DON'T HAVE TO WORRY ABOUT THAT ANYMORE, AMBER. EVERYTHING'S GOING TO BE ALRIGHT NOW.
YOUR MOM AND I ARE TAKING YOU TO A SAFE PLACE. WE'RE ALL GOING TO BE HAPPY THERE. YOU'LL SEE.
WE'RE GOING TO BE A FAMILY AGAIN.

KEEP AMBER IN THE CAR.
WHAT IS THAT?

OH, GOD...
AMBER, **STAY IN THE CAR!**
KYLE, IS THAT-- REVEREND ANDERSON?!
GOD, KYLE-- WHAT DID HE **DO?!**

I DON'T KNOW... JUST... KEEP AMBER IN THE CAR. JUST...

MOMMY, IS HE **DEAD?** IS THAT MAN--
DON'T LOOK, AMBER.

HE'S-- HE'S--
AAAAAHHHHH!!

Shiny NAILS
ORANGE KITCHEN
FOR ALL YOUR NEEDS
99¢ DISCOUNT
BEN'S PIZZA

Shiny NAILS
ORANGE KITCHEN
99¢ DIS
BEN'S PIZZA

WHAT
HAPPENED?

I HAD NO CHOICE. YOU'VE SEEN WHAT HE'S CAPABLE OF. YOU'VE SEEN WHAT WE'RE UP AGAINST.
THIS WAS THE ONLY WAY TO GET THE UPPER HAND--TO GET CONTROL OF THIS SITUATION.

JESUS, JOHN... YOU... I CAN'T BELIEVE YOU...

YOU MURDERED HIM?

...

MURDER?

YOU THINK THE DEVIL CAN BE MURDERED?! I HAVE SLAIN A VESSEL CORRUPTED BY PURE EVIL!
I HAVE RID THE WORLD OF AN AGENT OF DARKNESS HELL-BENT ON DESTROYING US!
I HAVE NOT COMMITTED THE SIN OF MURDER! THIS WAS NO MAN...
LOOK AT HIM!
DON'T YOU SEE THE BLACK FILTH FROM THE DEEPEST PITS OF HELL POURING OUT OF HIM?!
YOU CAN SEE HOW HIS SIN WAS ROTTING HIM INSIDE AND OUT.

DON'T TRY TO TELL ME THIS WAS A MAN WHO COULD BE MURDERED! I SAW WHAT HE WAS--YOU SAW WHAT HE WAS!
THIS CREATURE WAS FOAMING AT THE MOUTH WITH THE BLACK BILE OF SATAN WHILE HE SPEWED LIES AT ME--TRYING TO BREAK MY WILL.

HE SOUGHT TO CONTROL ME, AS HE HAS SO MANY OTHERS IN OUR TOWN--BUT WITH THE POWER OF THE LORD ON MY SIDE, HE DID NOT SUCCEED.

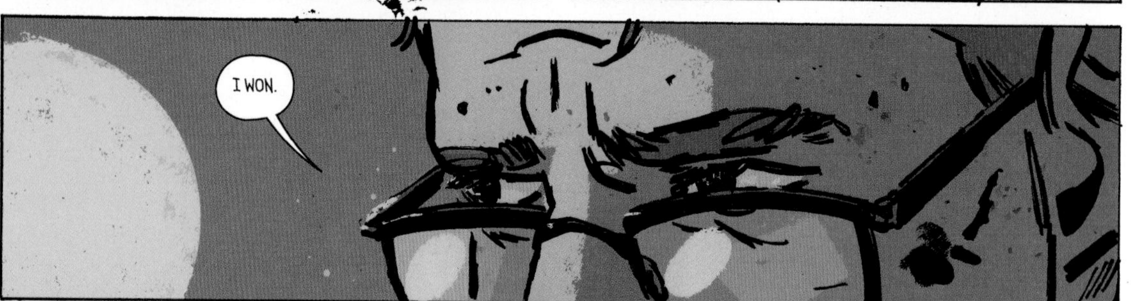
I WON.

KYLE.
JUSTIFY IT HOWEVER YOU WANT, REVEREND... IT DOESN'T CHANGE THE FACT THAT YOU'RE STANDING NEXT TO A DEAD BODY.
YOU'VE CROSSED A LINE HERE--THIS... THIS ISN'T WHAT WE SET OUT TO DO.
THIS ISN'T--

KYLE!
I CAN'T STAY HERE.
I KNOW.

GIVE ME THE KEYS, BRIAN.
KYLE, DON'T DO THIS.

KYLE, PLEASE... THIS IS... IT'S A GOOD THING. OUR WORK CAN CONTINUE AND HE WON'T INTERFERE.
THIS HAD TO HAPPEN FOR US TO SOLVE THIS THING. WE COULDN'T MOVE FORWARD WITHOUT--
DON'T LEAVE. NOT NOW. NOT AFTER THIS TRIUMPH. WE CAN'T DO THIS WITHOUT YOU.
JUST LOOK AT YOURSELF.
I CAN'T HAVE ANYTHING TO DO WITH THIS.

KYLE, IT'S NOT SAFE-- WHERE WILL YOU GO?
I'LL JUST KEEP DRIVING UNTIL PEOPLE STOP GIVING US A SECOND LOOK...

MOMMY, I'M *SCARED.*
I KNOW, BUT IT'S GOING TO BE OKAY, AMBER.

WE CAME HERE TO BE SAFE-- I FEEL **MORE** SCARED NOW.

WE'RE GOING TO BE SAFE. WE **ARE** SAFE, HONEY. I'M HERE... WE'RE ALL **TOGETHER NOW.** EVERYTHING IS GOING TO BE--
FUEL
E

WHAT, KYLE?
WHAT IS IT?

WE'VE GOT A PROBLEM.

THEY CAN SEE US, DADDY.
THEY CAN'T, AMBER. I PROMISE.
SKREEEEEEE
HEY! WHAT ARE YOU--?!
SWR-813

MOVE YOUR FUCKING CAR!
JEEZ, LADY— WHAT'S YOUR PROBLEM?
SKREEet
WHAT'S GOING ON HERE?
KYLE, NO!
STAY IN THE CAR, KIDDO.
GONNA HAVE TO ASK YOU TO COME WITH ME, BARNES.
WE CAN KEEP YOUR WIFE AND DAUGHTER SAFE WHILE YOU ANSWER OUR QUESTIONS...
THE HELL YOU WILL...
ICE

WHAT IF I HAVE PLANS FOR HIM?
Rebel
WHO THE FUCK ARE YOU?

YEEAAGGH!!

IS HE--?
I DON'T KNOW.

LET SCOTT GO!
STOP HIM!

WHAKOOM

POLICE

WHO--
I DON'T CARE--WE HAVE TO GET AMBER OUT OF HERE NOW.

YOU'RE IN THE WRONG TOWN, OUTCAST.

WHUD
WRAM

KOOM

WE HAVE TO GET THIS CAR MOVED--HE DIDN'T LEAVE THE KEYS IN IT.
KYLE?
KYLE?

KRAKK

WRAMM

KOOM

KRAKK

TOO WEAK--SO MANY...
NOT USED TO THIS MANY AT ONCE.
HELP-- HELP ME.
WHO ARE YOU?
SUNO
POLICE

I--
--I'M YOUR FATHER.

STOP.

YOU WAIT IN THE CAR.
YES, MR. STONE.

I DID NOT COME HERE TO STARE AT AN EMPTY CHAIR.
SIDNEY WAS RECKLESS, WE ALL KNEW THIS. FOR HIM TO NOT ARRIVE AFTER SO LONG WITHOUT ANY CONTACT WITH US...
HE MUST BE **DEAD.**

SURPRISED IT TOOK THIS LONG. HIS ACTIONS WERE FAR BEYOND WHAT WE **USUALLY** EMPLOY.

BECAUSE HE RECOGNIZED HOW **DIRE** THINGS HAVE GOTTEN. SIDNEY KNEW WE HAD TO MOVE FAST AND MAKE **BOLD** MOVES, OR THERE WOULD BE NO PROGRESS.

AND WHERE IS ALL THAT PROGRESS? KYLE BARNES IS YET **ANOTHER** OUTCAST TO SLIP THROUGH OUR GRASP.

WE DID NOT COME HERE TO DWELL ON OUR **FAILURES,** DID WE?
OUR GROUPS ARE INTACT AND GROWING... LET US ADDRESS **THAT.** WHO HAS IDENTIFIED A NEW OUTCAST SINCE OUR TIME APART?

KYLE, HELP HIM UP!
KYLE!
NEED TO... GO... MORE WILL COME.
GET SOMEPLACE...
...SAFE.
KYLE, WE NEED TO HELP HIM.
HE SAVED US. DON'T JUST STAND THERE.
...
POLICE

SECLUDED... NEED A PLACE... AWAY FROM PEOPLE.
I'M SORRY I CAN'T HELP YOU, SO MANY OF THEM, IT **DRAINS** ME. I'LL BE FINE... LEAVE ME.
I CAN...

OH MY GOD!
WHUDD

KYLE, WHAT ARE WE GOING TO--
HELP ME GRAB HIS FEET.
WE'RE BRINGING HIM?
I DON'T KNOW WHAT ELSE TO DO. WE CAN'T JUST **LEAVE** HIM HERE.
WHERE ARE WE TAKING HIM?
SAFE... WITH NO PEOPLE AROUND? I ONLY KNOW **ONE** PLACE...
NO... WE CAN'T...

YOU'RE BACK?
DID SOMETHING HAPPEN?

SOMETHING ELSE, YOU MEAN? REVEREND, PLEASE... JUST... KEEP YOUR DISTANCE.

KYLE, WHAT ARE WE GOING TO--
HELP ME GRAB HIS FEET.
WE'RE BRINGING HIM?
I DON'T KNOW WHAT ELSE TO DO. WE CAN'T JUST **LEAVE** HIM HERE.
WHERE ARE WE TAKING HIM?
SAFE... WITH NO PEOPLE AROUND? I ONLY KNOW **ONE** PLACE...
NO... WE CAN'T...

YOU'RE BACK?
DID SOMETHING HAPPEN?

SOMETHING ELSE, YOU MEAN? REVEREND, PLEASE... JUST... KEEP YOUR DISTANCE.

WHY'D YOU COME BACK?
WHAT'S GOING ON?

IT'S COMPLICATED-- I'LL GO INTO MORE DETAIL LATER, BUT IT'S **WORSE** OUT THERE THAN WE THOUGHT.
THIS IS OUR ONLY OPTION FOR NOW.
WHO IS THAT?
SWR-813
THAT'S ALSO COMPLICATED.
NO. I CAN'T **DO** THIS. I'M SORRY.

IF WE'RE STAYING, **HE GOES.**
I'M NOT GOING TO ALLOW MY DAUGHTER TO BE AROUND THAT MAN... NOT AFTER HE... NO MATTER HOW YOU JUSTIFY IT.
I'LL GO.
STOP.

THERE'S A... **BARN** AT THE BACK OF THE PROPERTY.
YOU CAN STAY THERE... AT LEAST UNTIL WE FIGURE THINGS OUT.

SUN
AMBULANCE
SUN
MV PLUMBING
THEY ARE NOT GOING TO BE HAPPY ABOUT THIS.

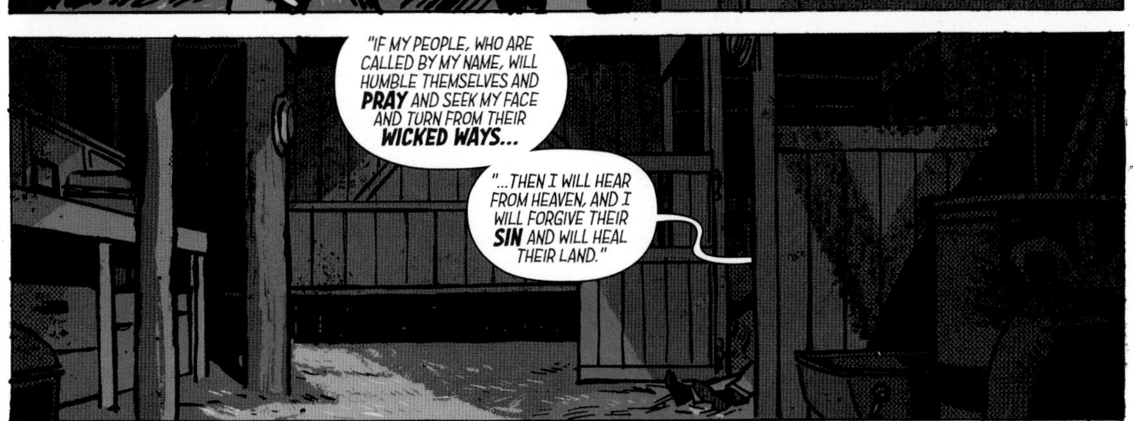
"IF MY PEOPLE, WHO ARE CALLED BY MY NAME, WILL HUMBLE THEMSELVES AND **PRAY** AND SEEK MY FACE AND TURN FROM THEIR **WICKED WAYS...**
"...THEN I WILL HEAR FROM HEAVEN, AND I WILL FORGIVE THEIR **SIN** AND WILL HEAL THEIR LAND."

I CAN TRY AND SNEAK INTO MY HOUSE... GET SOME MATTRESSES AT SOME POINT.
THIS IS FINE.

THE HELL IT IS. IF WE SPEND ANY LENGTH OF TIME HERE... I CAN'T HAVE YOU SLEEPING ON THE FLOOR.
I'M NOT WORRIED ABOUT BEING COMFORTABLE.
HOW IS SHE?
SHE HASN'T TAKEN NAPS IN A WHILE... BUT TODAY WAS... TODAY WAS A DAY. I DON'T KNOW HOW MUCH SHE SAW, BUT...

I NEVER WOULD HAVE BROUGHT YOU HERE IF I'D KNOWN...

IT'S OKAY. THOSE THINGS, WHATEVER THEY ARE, THEY'RE AFTER OUR GIRL. I HAVE TO BE HONEST, I HAVEN'T FELT AS SAFE AS I DO RIGHT NOW FOR DAYS.
AND...

SEEING SOMEONE FIGHT THEM... LIKE THAT MAN DID... IT WAS TERRIFYING IN THE MOMENT... BUT NOW, IT'S JUST...
THIS FLOOR IS NICE. I'LL TAKE THE FLOOR AND THIS FEELING OVER WHERE I WAS... ANY DAY OF THE WEEK.

DO YOU THINK HE'S REALLY YOUR FATHER?

I DON'T KNOW.
WHOEVER HE IS, HE'S MIXED UP IN ALL THIS... AND IT'S PRETTY SAFE TO SAY HE'S ON OUR SIDE.
THINGS ARE MOVING SO ***FAST.***

NOT ALL OF THEM IN A BAD DIRECTION.

SORRY ABOUT ALL THIS, KYLE.
THANK YOU FOR GETTING ME OUT OF THERE. YOU DIDN'T HAVE TO... I DIDN'T EXPECT YOU TO HELP ME.
YOU HELPED US... ONLY FAIR WE HELP YOU.

...

I DON'T EVEN KNOW YOUR **NAME.**

YOU CAN CALL ME SIMON... I DON'T... DAD WOULD PROBABLY FEEL WEIRD AT THIS POINT.

YOU THINK?

I'M SORRY I LEFT...
I HOPE YOU UNDERSTAND... IT WAS TO PROTECT--
THAT'S NOT WHAT I WANT TO TALK ABOUT... NOT RIGHT NOW.

HOW DID YOU DO ALL THAT TODAY? THOSE MEN, THEY WERE **MERGED,** RIGHT? AND YOU STILL... EXORCISED THEM.
I DIDN'T THINK YOU COULD GET THOSE THINGS OUT OF THEM AFTER A WHILE.

I CONDEMNED THOSE MEN TO THE PRISON OF THEIR OWN BODIES. WE CAN'T... **RECOVER** FROM THAT LEVEL OF PROLONGED EXPOSURE.
YOUR MOTHER...
I ONLY DO THAT IF I HAVE TO... IF THERE'S NO OTHER WAY.

SO THERE'S NO FIXING IT?
NOT THAT I'VE FOUND...
...BUT I DON'T KNOW EVERYTHING. WHAT I KNOW, I HAD TO FIGURE OUT ON MY OWN. I DON'T HAVE IT ALL WORKED OUT YET.
DON'T KNOW THAT I **EVER** WILL...
YOU CAN'T BLAME YOURSELF FOR WHAT HAPPENED TO YOUR MOTHER. IT WAS AN **ACCIDENT.**
IF I'D KNOWN... IF I'D STAYED... MAYBE I COULD HAVE...

WHY ARE YOU HERE NOW?
I'VE BEEN ON MY OWN... MOSTLY... AND I FEEL LIKE I'VE ACCOMPLISHED A LOT. I HAVE A **PLAN...** AND I KNOW HOW TO HURT THEM.
I'VE DONE AS MUCH AS I CAN ON MY OWN.

YOU'VE BEEN WATCHING ME? YOU KNEW WHERE I WAS?
I'VE CHECKED IN. ALWAYS KEPT MY DISTANCE.
I KNEW WHERE YOU WERE.

YOU KNOW HOW TO ***HURT*** THEM?

YES. ***SO DO YOU.***
RIGHT?

MY TOUCH, IT AFFECTS THEM... BUT NOT LIKE THAT. NOT LIKE YOU.
I DON'T HAVE ***THAT*** POWER.

YOU DO.
YOU JUST DON'T KNOW HOW TO HARNESS IT.

IT'S NOT YOUR TOUCH... IT'S YOUR ENERGY. YOU JUST HAVE ONLY USED IT THROUGH YOUR TOUCH.
WE, YOU AND I... AND OTHERS LIKE US, WE HAVE A PIECE OF THEIR WORLD, WHERE THEY COME FROM, IN US. WE'RE THE LIGHT TO THEIR DARKNESS. THEY LOST IT AND WE HAVE IT.
IT'S THAT ENERGY THAT AFFECTS THEM... THAT GIVES US POWER.
IT CAN BE DIRECTED, PUSHED, PULLED, STEERED AND INTENSIFIED ONCE YOU KNOW HOW TO RECOGNIZE IT.
YOU CAN DIRECT YOUR ENERGY AROUND, FOCUS IT INTO A WEAPON TO EXPAND THE REACH OF YOUR TOUCH... AND ITS POWER.
IT JUST TAKES CONCENTRATION.

SIMON...
...I'M SICK OF THE PEOPLE I LOVE CONSTANTLY BEING IN DANGER.

I NEED YOU TO TEACH ME **EVERYTHING** YOU KNOW.

POK
POK

POK
POK

POK

AMBER, WHAT ARE YOU DOING OUT HERE?

AMBER?
IS THE DEVIL BURIED HERE?

...

YES.

BUT, MOMMY, WHEN MOLLY CLIFFORD TOLD ME ABOUT THE DEVIL AND I GOT REAL SCARED AFTER SCHOOL, YOU TOLD ME THE DEVIL WASN'T REAL.
I WAS WRONG.

THEY ARE FROM A SPACE JUST BEYOND OUR REACH AND YET VERY CLOSE. MORE NEAR THAN WE COULD COMPREHEND, I'M TOLD.
IN THAT PLACE THEY EXIST ONLY AS ENERGY. THAT IS WHY LIFE HERE IS SO **APPEALING** TO THEM... THEY LONG FOR THE EXPERIENCE OF A PHYSICAL EXISTENCE.

IN THEIR REALM, THERE WERE TWO DIFFERENT KINDS OF ENERGIES, A LIGHT AND A DARK, A POSITIVE AND A NEGATIVE.
LONG AGO THEY LIVED IN A **PERFECT BALANCE.**

NOBODY KNOWS WHAT, BUT SOMETHING HAPPENED AND THAT BALANCE WAS BROKEN FOREVER.
THE NEGATIVE STARTED TO OVERPOWER THE POSITIVE.

WHAT THEN ENSUED, I'M TOLD, WAS THE LARGEST, MOST VIOLENT CONFLICT TO EVER TAKE PLACE.
IT WOULD HAVE RIPPED OUR WORLD APART--IN FACT, IT EVENTUALLY RIPPED THROUGH THE BARRIER BETWEEN OUR WORLDS--ALLOWING THIS ENERGY TO ESCAPE.

ONCE HERE, IT BONDED WITH HUMANITY, MUCH THE SAME WAY YOU'VE EXPERIENCED THE **NEGATIVE** ENERGY BONDING WITH PEOPLE NOW.

IT WAS A DIFFERENT... MORE **HARMONIOUS** UNION. THOSE WITH IT CONSIDERED IT A GIFT, AND IT WAS A GIFT THEY PASSED DOWN TO THEIR DESCENDANTS, THE SAME WAY I PASSED IT TO YOU...

...AND YOU PASSED IT TO AMBER.

WHAT I HAVE TAUGHT YOU--IS HOW TO **HONE** THAT POWER... TO FOCUS IT, TO DIRECT IT.

YOU STILL HAVE MUCH TO LEARN, BUT THIS IS AS FAR AS I CAN TAKE YOU HERE--TO GO FURTHER WE'D NEED TO VENTURE OUT--PUT OURSELVES AT RISK MORE.

I'M WILLING TO DO WHATEVER I HAVE TO DO SO WE CAN END THIS.
OKAY, THEN.
I KNOW THIS HAS BEEN A ROUGH FEW MONTHS, BUT THIS WILL BE WORTH IT. TOGETHER... I THINK WE CAN BRING A STOP TO IT ALL.
ON YOUR FEET.

OKAY, GO.
THHOOM
GOOD.
AGAIN.
THOOM
OKAY... THAT WAS THE MOST POWERFUL ONE, YET.
YOU'VE REALLY TAKEN TO THIS QUICKER THAN ANYONE ELSE I'VE TRAINED.
HOW MANY OTHERS?
NOT ENOUGH. OKAY. AGAIN.

NEED HELP?
GILES AND ALLISON ARE GETTING THE REST.

SORRY, I WAS DOWNSTAIRS TRAINING.

HOW DID I KNOW THAT? OH YEAH--IT'S BECAUSE THAT'S ALL YOU'VE BEEN FUCKING DOING SINCE YOU CAME TO THIS SHITHOLE ON THE ASS-END OF THE COUNTY.

I MISS YOU, TOO, SIS.

THAT'S RIGHT--WE'RE FAMILY... AND FAMILY SNEAKS A COUPLE COUNTIES OVER AND DRIVES GROCERIES TO YOUR SECRET HIDEOUT WHETHER THEY WANT TO OR NOT.
I DO HAVE A JOB, Y'KNOW.

AUNT MEGAN IS HERE!

HELL YEAH, SHE IS!
MEGAN!

SORRY, SORRY. DON'T TALK LIKE AUNT MEGAN, HONEY.
DID YOU BRING HOLLY?

OH, I'M SORRY, HONEY... SHE'S IN SCHOOL RIGHT NOW.

I'LL BRING HER AGAIN, I PROMISE.
I WISH I COULD GO TO SCHOOL.

AMBER, HONEY... YOU KNOW WE CAN'T DO THAT... NOT UNTIL THE PEOPLE STOP WATCHING YOU. AND DADDY... HE'S GOING TO FIX THAT.
I **HATE** IT HERE.

I CAN TALK TO HER.
WE NEED TO GO.

WHAT? WHERE ARE WE GOING?

I'VE TAUGHT YOU AS MUCH AS I CAN HERE. THE REST OF YOUR TRAINING WILL HAVE TO BE ON THE ROAD.
PLEASE. WE CAN'T WASTE ANY MORE TIME.

GO.
THIS IS WHAT WE'RE HERE FOR.

SIMON, TAKE CARE OF HIM.
ALWAYS. WE MAY BE GONE 'TIL TOMORROW. DON'T WAIT UP.

NEVER A DULL FUCKING MOMENT.

SO HE'S JUST OUT THERE, LIVING IN THE BARN?
YEAH, I BRING HIM FOOD EVERY MORNING... WE TALK A LITTLE. HE'S NOT A BAD-- I'LL-- I'LL DROP IT.
AMBER OKAY?
YES. NO. I DON'T KNOW. I NEVER KNOW. I FEEL LIKE THE WORST MOTHER PRETTY MUCH ALL DAY, EVERY DAY.
SO THAT'S FUN.
YOU'VE SEEN THINGS... YOU KNOW WHAT YOU'RE DOING IS RIGHT. THIS IS... WELL, IT'S LIFE DURING WARTIME. IT'S NOT NORMAL, IT'S NOT FUN... AND KIDS, KIDS ARE RESILIENT.
THIS WILL MAKE HER STRONGER.
I HOPE YOU'RE RIGHT. AS FUCKED UP AS THIS IS, BEING WITH HER FATHER, THAT'S A BIG DEAL. THAT'S BEEN GREAT. I'VE REALLY SEEN A CHANGE IN HER BECAUSE OF THAT.
TRUTH BE TOLD, IT'S BEEN GREAT FOR ME, TOO... BEING BACK TOGETHER.
BEING ABLE TO MAKE SENSE OF WHAT DROVE US APART IN THE FIRST PLACE.
WE'RE BOTH HAPPIER.
SOUNDS THAT WAY. I MEAN--SHIT. THE WALLS IN THIS OLD HOUSE AREN'T VERY THICK.
OKAY. JESUS.
SORRY.
JESUS.

WHAT THE--

WHAT? WHAT IS IT?
I THOUGHT I SAW SOMETHING.
THERE WAS SOMEONE... NEAR THE BARN.

THE BARN? PROBABLY JUST ANDERSON GOING FOR A WALK.

YEAH.

WHAT IS THIS PLACE?
I CAME TO YOU WHEN I DID BECAUSE I NEED YOUR HELP. I WANTED TO KEEP YOU OUT OF THIS FOR AS LONG AS I COULD... BUT I KNEW I COULDN'T GO FURTHER WITHOUT YOU.
IT'S TIME WE MADE THEM FEAR US. ARE YOU READY?
READY? READY FOR WHAT?

YOU'LL SEE.

THERE'S...
THERE'S SO MANY OF THEM.

AND YET LOOK AT THEM. THEY COWER AT THE SIGHT OF US. THEY SLINK TO THEIR SHADOWS IN THE HOPES WE WON'T DARE FOLLOW. THEY **KNOW** THE POWER WE HAVE.
DO YOU?
I **DO.**
GO. USE WHAT YOU HAVE LEARNED. YOU KNOW WHAT TO DO.
DO WHAT WE WERE PUT ON THIS EARTH TO DO.

SAVE THEM.

HM.
301·3BK

UNLESS THEY ARE BOTH ACCOMPLISHED LIARS, YOUR HUSBAND AND DAUGHTER HAVE PROVEN YOU'RE THE ONLY ONE WHO CAN GIVE US THE INFORMATION WE DEMAND.
WHERE IS KYLE BARNES?

LEAVE MY FAMILY ALONE AND GET THE FUCK OUT OF MY HOUSE.
NOW!

YOUR HOUSE. YOUR LOVELY HOUSE.
LET ME TELL YOU SOMETHING YOU PROBABLY ALREADY KNOW ABOUT THIS HOME.
FLAK
FLIK
IT WOULD BURN. WOULDN'T EVEN TAKE MUCH. OLD WIRING--COULD BE ANYTHING THAT STARTS THE FIRE. NO ONE WOULD BE TO BLAME.
MAYBE YOU'RE ALL INSIDE WHEN THE FLAMES COME. MAYBE YOU'RE UNABLE TO GET OUT.

I'LL LEAVE YOU TO THINK THINGS OVER.
KYLE BARNES.
DECIDE WHICH FAMILY YOU LOVE MORE...

...BEFORE YOU LOSE BOTH.
MARK...

I COULDN'T, MEGAN... I COULDN'T STOP THEM.
I'M SO SORRY.
IT'S OKAY... IT'S NOT YOUR FAULT.

ARE THEY GONE?
YES. WHAT IS THE UPDATE?
I DROVE ALL OVER TODAY... STILL NO SIGN OF THEM. SURELY THEY MUST HAVE LEFT THE STATE, RIGHT?
CALEB, PLEASE. DO YOU SERIOUSLY THINK WE'RE ONLY LOOKING FOR THEM **HERE?**
WE ARE LOOKING FOR THEM EVERYWHERE WE HAVE **EYES.**
AND WE HAVE EYES **EVERYWHERE.**
INDEED, WE DO, REVEREND POLK.
GLAD TO SEE YOUR CONGREGATION BEING SO ACCEPTING OF YOU SO QUICKLY. THIS COMMUNITY IS VERY RAPIDLY SWAYING TO OUR SIDE.
IT IS ONLY A MATTER OF TIME BEFORE KYLE BARNES IS FLUSHED OUT INTO THE OPEN.

GOOD NIGHT, HONEY. I LOVE YOU.
MOM, I KNOW WE'RE SAFE HERE... BUT I'M STILL SCARED.

IT'S OKAY TO BE SCARED... SOMETIMES WE JUST CAN'T HELP IT. AS LONG AS YOU KNOW THAT YOU ARE SAFE HERE AND THAT YOU DON'T **NEED** TO BE SCARED.
THE BAD PEOPLE CAN'T GET US HERE.

MOM, IS DAD REALLY GOING TO BE ABLE TO MAKE THE BAD PEOPLE GO AWAY FOR GOOD?

YES, HONEY... THAT'S WHAT HE'S OUT THERE DOING RIGHT NOW...

IT'S NOT WORKING!
YOU'RE NOT FOCUSED.
WRAKK
WRAMM
AAAGH!
WRAKK

FTHWOOM

WROK

KLUNK
AAAGH!

SIMON!
WRAMM

YOU DON'T NEED TO SEE THEM--YOU SHOULD **FEEL** THEM AROUND YOU.

WHOOM
GET UP!
I CAN'T DO THIS ALONE!
WROK

C'MON!

I'M OKAY.
I'M READY.

KRAK
WOULDN'T MATTER IF YOU **WEREN'T.**

THWOOM
FWOOM
THOOM
THIS ISN'T OVER.
COME ON...

OH, GOD--
OUR WORK HERE IS JUST BEGINNING...

A LITTLE HELP?

YOU GOTTA BE MORE CAREFUL OUT HERE WITH ALL THIS SHIT. ALLISON SAW ONE OF YOUR... CONGREGATION.
IF THEY FIND OUT WHAT YOU'RE DOING--THEY WON'T BE HAPPY.

NOW WHY ON EARTH WOULD THEY BE UNHAPPY WITH WHAT I'M DOING?

WE'RE ALL HIDING OUT HERE, REVEREND.
WE SHOULDN'T BE DRAWING ATTENTION TO OURSELVES. YOU KNOW THIS IS A RISK.

DRAWING ATTENTION TO OURSELVES? IS THAT WHAT YOU THINK I'M DOING?
HEH...
HA! HA! HA! HA! HA! HA!
...

YOU THINK I DON'T KNOW WHAT'S GOING ON IN THERE? KYLE'S FATHER'S BACK--THIS SIMON FELLA YOU TOLD ME ABOUT. HE'S TRAINING KYLE ON HOW BETTER TO USE HIS ABILITIES... SOON WE'LL HAVE TWO OF THEM... BETTER THAN KYLE EVER WAS ON HIS OWN.
MEANWHILE, THE WORLD BEYOND THIS FARM IS GOING TO SHIT-- AND WHEN THEY'RE READY, THOSE BOYS ARE GOING TO CONFRONT IT HEAD-ON.
SO, YEAH... I'M DRAWING A BIT OF ATTENTION TO US...

BECAUSE I'M GATHERING A RIGHTEOUS ARMY.

AS MANY OF YOU KNOW, I DISCOVERED YOU AT MY LOWEST POINT. I WAS AT THE ABSOLUTE **BOTTOM.** I'D LOST MY HOME, MY CHURCH, MY COMMUNITY... AND MY FRIENDS.

IT SEEMED THE WHOLE WORLD HAD TURNED AGAINST ME... BECAUSE IT **HAD.**

SO THAT I CAN BASK IN THE WARMTH OF HIS SUN, UNASHAMED AND UNJUDGED...
...CELEBRATED, EVEN...
FOR WHAT I'VE DONE AND WHAT I'VE LIVED THROUGH.

FOR THIS IS NOT A FLOCK OF SHEEP I STAND BEFORE NOW--YOU ARE LIONS!
AND YOU SIT BEFORE ME WITH YOUR EYES OPEN TO THE EVILS OF THE WORLD!

YOU CAN FEEL IT--ALL AROUND US, BUILDING--THREATENING TO SWALLOW US WHOLE!
THE DARKNESS I HAVE FACED HEAD-ON--THAT MARKED ME--IS HERE, AND IT IS REAL!
WE DO NOT FEAR IT! WE DO NOT PRETEND IT IS NOT THERE! WE PREPARE! WE STRENGTHEN OURSELVES WITH THE WORD OF OUR LORD AND SAVIOR!
FOR SOON WE WILL FACE THIS DARKNESS IN BATTLE!

THANK YOU ALL FOR COMING. I HOPE TO SEE EVEN MORE OF YOU NEXT WEEK.
THEY ALL CHECK OUT, KYLE?
I DIDN'T SEE ANY REACTIONS TO MY PRESENCE--I'D WAGER THEY'RE ALL CLEAN.
WHERE'D YOU FIND ALL THESE PEOPLE, REVEREND?
IT'S GOOD TO BE TALKING TO YOU AGAIN, TOO, KYLE. THE FARM NEXT DOOR HAD A TENT CHURCH... SHORT A REVEREND, TOO. BARN CHURCH BEATS TENT CHURCH IN THE GAME OF TENT, BARN, ROCK.
ALMOST LIKE GOD PLANNED IT.
YOU THINK THIS IS SAFE?
SAFETY IN NUMBERS, RIGHT?
MORE COMING EVERY WEEK. COULD USE YOUR HELP--VETTING THEM ALL. SOMEONE TO MAKE SURE THERE AREN'T ANY SNAKES IN OUR MIDST.

YOU NEED TO STOP ALL THIS.

I'M AFRAID THERE'S NOTHING YOU COULD EVER DO TO GET ME TO STOP BEING A **SERVANT OF THE LORD,** KYLE.

THAT'S **EXACTLY** WHAT I'M TALKING ABOUT. THERE IS NO GOD. YOU CAN STOP THIS.
QUIT TORTURING YOURSELF AND GO FIND YOUR SON. GO BACK TO YOUR LIFE--QUIT... **WASTING** IT.

KYLE...

I WOULD APPRECIATE YOU NOT USING PERSONAL THINGS I'VE TOLD YOU IN CONFIDENCE TO GET A RISE OUT OF ME.
IT'S UNKIND.

I'M SORRY, IT'S JUST--YOU KNOW MY FATHER HAS BEEN TRAINING ME. HE'S ALSO BEEN FILLING IN SOME OF THE BLANKS, THINGS WE COULDN'T FIGURE OUT ON OUR OWN.
HE KNOWS **WHY** OUR POWERS WORK. HE KNOWS WHAT THESE THINGS **ARE.**
AND IT'S **NOT** WHAT YOU THINK.
OKAY THEN, KYLE... WHY DON'T YOU TELL ME WHAT YOU KNOW?

SO YOU SAY THEY'RE FROM ANOTHER PLANE OF EXISTENCE?
THAT'S WHAT HE SAYS, YES... AND IT ALL LINES UP WITH THINGS SIDNEY SAID TO ME, ABOUT ME BEING FROM THE SAME PLACE AS THEM.
IT'S SOME OTHER DIMENSION.
LIKE HELL?
NO, THAT'S EXACTLY WHAT I'M NOT SAYING.
YOU SAID THIS PLACE WAS "CLOSER THAN WE CAN COMPREHEND." I'VE HEARD IT SAID THERE IS A LITTLE BIT OF HELL INSIDE US ALL.
WE MAKE OUR OWN HELL, THINGS LIKE THAT.

HOW CAN YOU HEAR WHAT I'VE JUST TOLD YOU AND STILL SAY WORDS LIKE "HELL"?
CAN'T YOU SEE YOUR ENTIRE BELIEF SYSTEM IS BUILT ON A MISUNDERSTANDING THAT LED TO A LOT OF ASSUMPTIONS?
KYLE, PLEASE.

LET'S BE REAL HERE. WE'VE KNOWN EACH OTHER A VERY LONG TIME, AND YOU ARE SOMEONE I CONSIDER A FRIEND.
NO MATTER HOW MUCH DISTANCE OUR ACTIONS HAVE PUT BETWEEN US.
BUT YOU ARE A MAN WITHOUT FAITH. THAT HAS ALWAYS BEEN TRUE ABOUT YOU.

IT'S EASY FOR YOU TO TAKE WHAT YOU HEARD AND USE IT TO REAFFIRM YOUR SKEPTICISM. THAT IS YOUR MINDSET, THAT'S THE CORNER FROM WHICH YOU APPROACH THINGS.
YOU HEAR THESE THINGS AND YOU LINE THEM UP WITH YOUR ALREADY ESTABLISHED OPINIONS... YOU USE YOUR CONCLUSIONS TO SHAPE WHAT IT IS YOUR FATHER SAID TO YOU.
BIBLE
TO MY EAR--YOU JUST TOLD ME SOME OF THE SAME STORIES I'VE BEEN HEARING MY ENTIRE LIFE.
YOU JUST USED DIFFERENT WORDS.

YOU SAY "NEGATIVE ENTITY"...
...ALL I HEAR IS DEMON.
AND, KYLE...
... THAT MAKES YOU AN ANGEL.

I'M SORRY, KYLE...
...BUT IT'S JUST NOT **SAFE** FOR US OUT THERE ANYMORE.

AMBULANCE
POLICE
SIR, YOU CAN'T--

EXCUSE *ME?*
OF COURSE, SORRY, SIR-- GO RIGHT AHEAD.

MY WORD...
EMS
MEDIC

YOU DIDN'T NEED TO COME HERE. WE ARE DOING WHAT WE CAN TO MANAGE THIS.
MANAGE? THERE IS NO WAY OF **MANAGING** THIS, MR. STONE.
THOSE WHO WEREN'T YET MERGED HAVE BEEN REUNITED WITH THEIR FAMILIES. THEY'RE TELLING STORIES OF BEING **DRUGGED--** MISSING TIME.
THEY LED THE POLICE HERE BEFORE WE COULD GET INVOLVED. BEFORE WE COULD **HIDE** THESE POOR SOULS... NOW **THEIR** FAMILIES ARE BEING CONTACTED.
MEDIC

THERE IS--
KOFF! KOFF! KOFF!
THIS WILL BE PUBLIC. THE NEWS CREWS ARE ALREADY ON THEIR WAY.
WE **CAN'T** CONTAIN THIS.

I'M SORRY. I GOT HERE AS SOON AS I COULD. I SCRAMBLED TO GET PEOPLE HERE. WE GOT CONTROL OF THE CRIME SCENE... I TRIED TO--
STOP.
IT'S TOO LATE FOR THAT NOW.

WE HAVE TO BE PREPARED FOR WHAT COMES **NEXT.** THEY WILL BE **EMBOLDENED** AFTER THIS.
THIS IS ONLY THE BEGINNING.
WE CAN INCREASE SECURITY AT ALL THE SAFE HOUSES IN THE AREA... BUT THERE'S NO WAY TO KNOW WHAT THEIR PLANS ARE, OR EVEN **IF** THEY'LL HIT US AGAIN ANYTIME SOON.
OH, THEY WILL... YOU'LL SEE...
MEDIC
MEDIC
...AND WE'LL BE **READY** FOR THEM.

WHAT? HOW?
I KNOW **EXACTLY** WHAT THEIR NEXT TARGET WILL BE...

LOOK HOW HAPPY THEY ARE.
...TWENTY MILES OUT OF CHARLESTON, A GRISLY SCENE AS POLICE INVESTIGATE WHAT IS BEING CALLED A "DRUG CULT." OVER A DOZEN PEOPLE WHO HAD BEEN ABDUCTED AND KEPT DRUGGED ARE NOW HOME WITH THEIR FAMILIES.
THEIR ABDUCTORS WERE FOUND CATATONIC ON THE SCENE AS MYSTERY UPON MYSTERY BEGINS TO STACK UP.

WAS THIS YOU AND SIMON?

YEAH.

THAT SEEMS LIKE PROGRESS.
RIGHT? IT FEELS GOOD.

GO LONG!
MONSTER SQUAD
YOU TWO PLAY CATCH WHILE I TALK TO AMBER'S DADDY FOR A BIT.
LOOKS LIKE IT MADE THE NEWS. THEY COULDN'T COVER IT UP.
THAT'S INTERESTING. MAYBE THEY'RE LESS ORGANIZED THAN WE REALIZE? MAYBE YOUR FRIEND'S GRISLY ACTIONS HAVE THEM IN DISARRAY.
NO MATTER WHAT IT IS... I THINK WE SHOULD WORK QUICKLY, TAKE ADVANTAGE OF WHATEVER IS GOING ON.
YOU READY TO DO IT **AGAIN?**
FOR **THEM?**
OF COURSE I AM.

HOW YOU HOLDING UP?
HOW DO YOU FUCKING THINK?

I'M SORRY, CHIEF. I DIDN'T MEAN TO STARTLE. I JUST... I DON'T HAVE TO BULLSHIT YOU, YOU KNOW? I'VE BEEN PUTTING ON A BRAVE FACE FOR MEGAN ALL THIS TIME.
OR TRYING TO, AT LEAST.

I'M NOT GOING TO PRETEND I'M OKAY. A MONSTER MADE MY WIFE THROW ME OUT OF A WINDOW, AND NOW I CAN'T WALK.
WHERE THE FUCK DO YOU GO FROM THERE?

HIDING OUT IN A FARM IN THE WOODS, IT SEEMS.
I KNOW IT'S HARD. I CAN'T PRETEND TO KNOW WHAT IT IS YOU'RE GOING THROUGH.

BUT AT LEAST YOU STILL HAVE MEGAN.
THOSE THINGS, THEY STILL HAVE ROSE. SHE'S ONE OF THEM... AND THE MORE TERRIFYING THOUGHT IS...
...MAYBE SHE ALWAYS WAS.

YOU REVEREND ANDERSON?
...OF OUR LORD'S HOLY CHURCH OF THE CREEPY BARN. AT YOUR SERVICE.
WHAT CAN I DO FOR YOU, YOUNG MAN?

MY NAME IS LOGAN ROSS. I WAS THERE AT THE GAS STATION THAT DAY KYLE BARNES DISAPPEARED. I SAW WHAT THAT MAN DID TO THOSE OTHERS.
SIR... I SAW THE **DEMONS** COME OUT OF THEM.
EVERYONE IN TOWN THINKS I'M CRAZY. NO ONE BELIEVES ME.

I BELIEVE YOU, LOGAN.

STEP INTO MY OFFICE.
LET'S HAVE US A TALK.

RISE & SHINE
ANY IDEA WHAT WE'RE UP AGAINST HERE?
THIS PLACE IS **BIGGER,** USED MORE REGULARLY BY MORE OF THEM.
ANOTHER THING, UNLESS THEIR SIDE HAS COMPLETELY BROKEN DOWN... THEY'RE GOING TO KNOW WE WERE COMING **HERE.**

THEY'RE PROBABLY **READY** FOR US.
HOW? WHY?

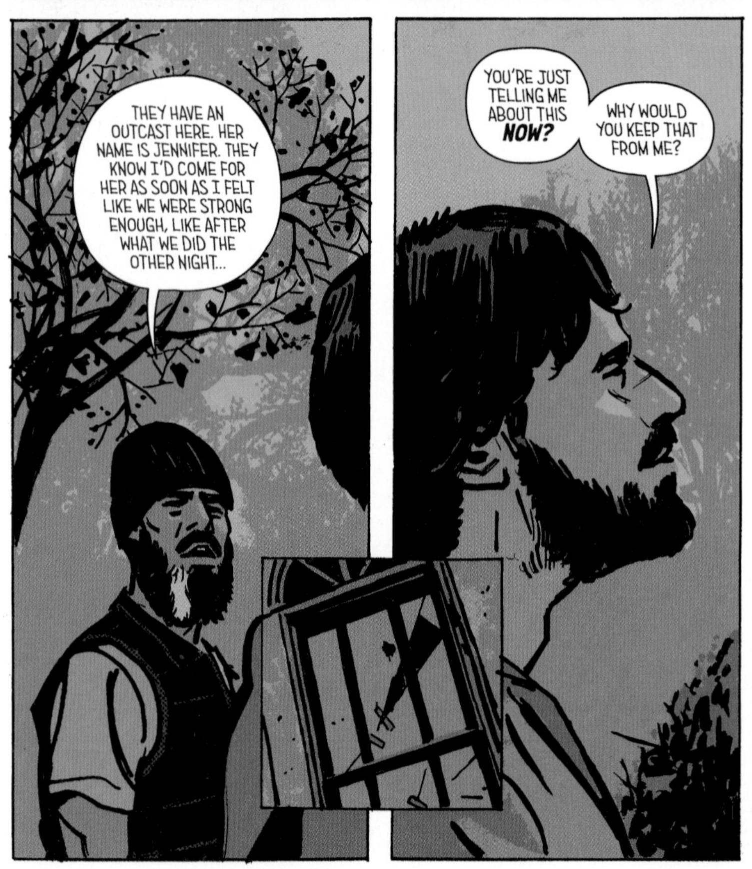
THEY HAVE AN OUTCAST HERE. HER NAME IS JENNIFER. THEY KNOW I'D COME FOR HER AS SOON AS I FELT LIKE WE WERE STRONG ENOUGH, LIKE AFTER WHAT WE DID THE OTHER NIGHT...
YOU'RE JUST TELLING ME ABOUT THIS **NOW?**
WHY WOULD YOU KEEP THAT FROM ME?

WOULD YOU HAVE BEEN ABLE TO FOCUS ON YOUR TRAINING IF YOU KNEW A FRIEND OF MINE WAS BEING HELD AGAINST THEIR WILL?
WOULD YOU HAVE **RUSHED?** HOPING TO RESCUE HER SOONER?
I HAD TO BE SURE WE COULD DO THIS RIGHT.

I'M SORRY.
DON'T BE.
WRAK
THEY'VE BARRICADED THE DOOR. THEY WANT US TO COME AROUND THE BACK.
ONE WAY IN... ONE WAY **OUT.**
ARE YOU SURE I'M READY FOR THIS?
I NEED **YOU** TO BE SURE YOU'RE READY FOR THIS.

I DON'T LIKE THIS **AT ALL.**
SHOULD WE WAIT?
FOR WHAT? IT'LL BE DARK SOON. I DON'T WANT TO GIVE THEM TIME TO PACK EVERYTHING UP AND MOVE SOMEWHERE I DON'T KNOW ABOUT.
LET'S GO.

BRAVE TO ENTER HERE.
FUNNY.
YOU LOOK LIKE THE BRAVE ONES TO US.

STAY FOCUSED.
LOOK OUT!
WRAKK

NEED YOU ALIVE... BUT JUST BAR--
AAAAGH!

DON'T LET THEM DISTRACT YOU!

WRAKK
YOU WILL NEVER LEAVE HERE.
YOU'RE SERVING THE GREAT MERGE UP TO US ON A PLATTER.
I DON'T THINK SO.
KYLE!

I CAN'T DO THIS WITHOUT YOU!
WRAMM

C'MON!
THE DOOR TO THE BASEMENT-- THEY'RE GUARDING IT!
ON IT.

THAT'S IT!
WHUDD
GOOD! **FOLLOW ME!**
WRAMM

OH, GOD!
DON'T LET THEIR NUMBERS SCARE YOU! WE CAN DO THIS!

REALLY?! HOW?
ONCE WE GET TO JENNIFER-- SHE'S ALMOST AS POWERFUL AS ME.
WITH HER WE'LL BE UNSTOPPABLE.
WRAMM

THIS MUST BE IT.

HOLD THEM OFF!
WRAKK
OH, GOD...
JENNIFER...

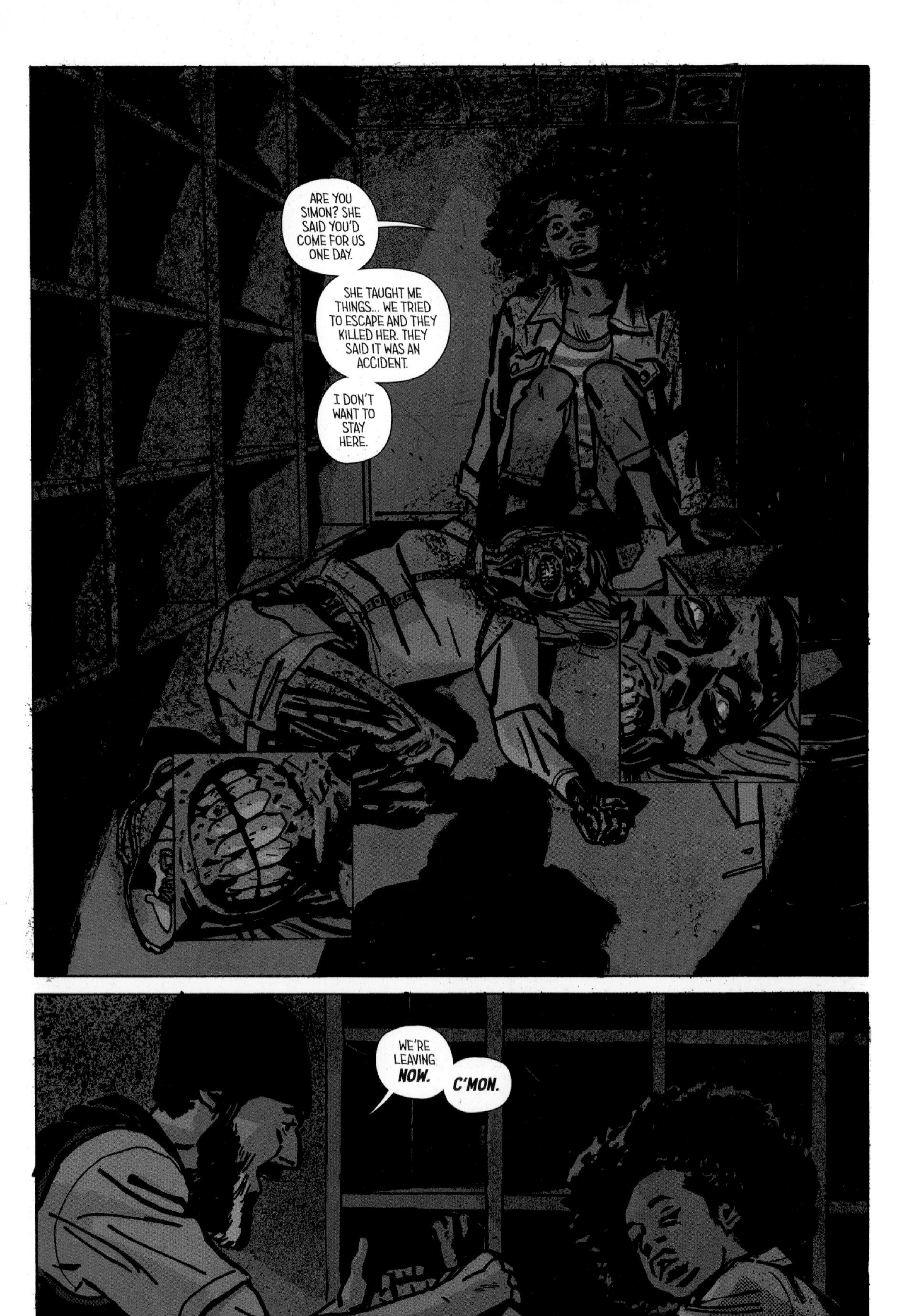
ARE YOU SIMON? SHE SAID YOU'D COME FOR US ONE DAY.
SHE TAUGHT ME THINGS... WE TRIED TO ESCAPE AND THEY KILLED HER. THEY SAID IT WAS AN ACCIDENT.
I DON'T WANT TO STAY HERE.
WE'RE LEAVING **NOW.**
C'MON.

IS THAT JENNIFER?
NO.
WHAT IS YOUR NAME, MA'AM?
DAPHNE.
THIS IS GOING TO BE SCARY, BUT IF YOU STAY BEHIND US, YOU'LL BE OKAY.
GOT IT?

WRAM
YOU CAN DO THIS.
JENNIFER SHOWED ME SOME THINGS.

OF COURSE SHE DID.

THIS WAY-- WE CAN MAKE IT!
NO!
THERE'S SO MANY PEOPLE HERE WHO AREN'T MERGED YET! WE HAVE TO SAVE THEM BEFORE IT'S TOO LATE!
WE HAVE TO STAY.
WE HAVE TO FIGHT!
WE CAN'T AFFORD THE RISK!
NO! HE'S RIGHT!
THE THREE OF US TOGETHER-- IT'S MAKING US STRONGER!
WRAKK

KRAKK
WRAMM
WHUDD

CREEK LODGE
TELL ME.
WE WERE ABLE TO CONTAIN IT. THE PEOPLE THEY SAVED HAVE NO MEMORY OF WHERE THEY WERE OR FOR HOW LONG.
THE PUBLIC WILL NEVER KNOW ABOUT THIS ONE. IT WON'T BE TIED TO THE OTHER STORY.
BUT THEY GOT AWAY... AND THEY TOOK THE GIRL.

HOW MANY DID WE LOSE?! HOW MANY DID YOU THROW AT THEM?!
THIS SHOULD HAVE BEEN **EASY!**
THEY SHOULD BE TIED UP NEXT TO THAT GIRL IN THE ROOM--GETTING US ONE STEP CLOSER TO THE MERGE! INSTEAD, WE ARE **FARTHER THAN EVER!**

DO YOU HAVE ANY IDEA WHAT YOU'VE--
SIR, PLEASE-- **CALM DOWN.**

KOFF
COUGH
HAKK
KOFF
KAFF
KOFF

KAFF
HAKK
KAFF
HAKK
KOFF
KAK
HIK
KOFF
HAKK

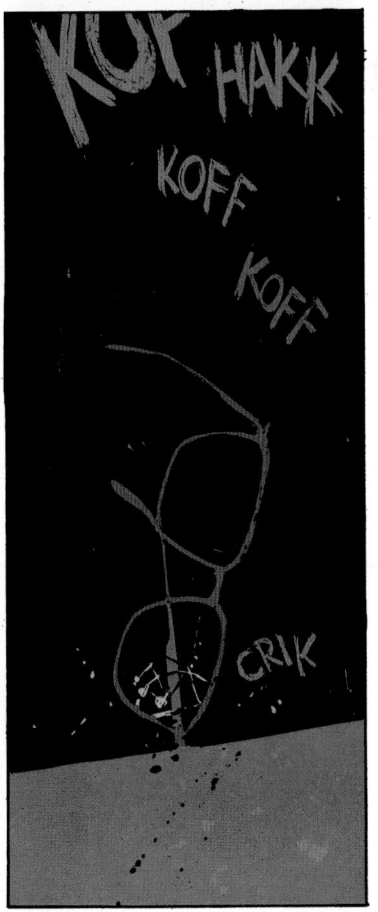
HAKK
KOFF
KOFF
CRIK

GOD...
...DAMN IT.

YOU GOING TO BE OKAY?
THINK SO.

WHAT THE HELL WAS **THAT?** WHY ARE WE SO TIRED--I FEEL LIKE I'VE BEEN JOGGING FOR FOUR DAYS, I--
THIS SUCKS! DID WE DO SOMETHING WRONG?

WE DRAW ON EACH OTHER'S POWER IN THE MOMENT, BUT THAT DOESN'T LAST... WE DID A LOT BACK THERE... SAVED A GREAT MANY PEOPLE.
THAT DRAINS US...
WE JUST...

...NEED TO REST FOR A MOMENT.
I HAVE TO STOP. I'M SORRY.

HUFF!
HUFF!
HUFF!

IT'S NOT **SAFE** OUT THERE--**GET HER INTO THE CAR!**
I'M TRYING!

GET BACK!
I DON'T KNOW YOU! YOU COULD HAVE DRUGGED ME! JENNIFER AND I TRIED TO ESCAPE ONCE--THIS DIDN'T HAPPEN AFTER THAT!
LOOK AT ME! WE'RE BOTH EXHAUSTED, TOO!
DID WE ALSO DRUG OURSELVES?
YOU HAVE EVERY REASON TO BE SCARED. I UNDERSTAND THAT. I CAN'T EVEN IMAGINE WHAT YOU'VE BEEN THROUGH. I'M SORRY FOR ALL OF THAT... BUT I PROMISE YOU, IT'S OVER NOW.
I KNOW YOU CAN FEEL A CONNECTION TO US. TRUST THAT.
LET'S GET BACK IN THE CAR.
WE'RE TAKING YOU SOMEPLACE SAFE.
BCZ 412

SHE CAN'T STAY HERE! WE HAVE NO IDEA WHO SHE IS!
I WON'T HAVE HER SLEEPING IN THE SAME HOUSE AS MY DAUGHTER. WE CAME HERE TO BE **SAFE.**

SHE'S ONE OF **US.** HAVING HER HERE MAKES US **SAFER.** YOU HAVE TO TRUST US ON THIS, MEGAN.
TRUST WHO, HIM? I'VE BARELY EVEN SPOKEN TO YOUR LONG-LOST FATHER!

TRUST ME, GODDAMNIT.
YOU THINK I'D EVER ENDANGER HOLLY? OR AMBER?
ALLISON, TELL HER.

KYLE...
I DON'T KNOW...

WHAT?

IT'S JUST... IT'S GETTING TO BE A LOT. YOU'VE GOT SIMON HERE, THERE'S AN UNMARKED GRAVE OUTSIDE, ANDERSON HAS A BARN FULL OF PEOPLE AT THE EDGE OF THE PROPERTY... AND NOW THIS?
I WORRY THINGS ARE GETTING OUT OF HAND.

I'M SORRY... YOU SEEM LIKE YOU MIGHT BE A NICE GIRL, BUT...

UNMARKED GRAVE? SOMEONE IS BURIED HERE?
I THINK... I THINK I'VE HEARD ENOUGH.

DAPHNE, DON'T--

IF YOU HAD ANY CLUE WHAT THAT POOR GIRL HAS LIVED THROUGH, YOU'D BE REALLY DISGUSTED WITH YOURSELVES RIGHT NOW.
FUCK.
I'M ALL EARS, KYLE...

DON'T LISTEN TO THEM. THEY NEED YOU. **WE** NEED YOU.
IT'S JUST GOING TO TAKE THEM A MINUTE TO REALIZE IT.
KYLE'S WORKING ON IT.

WHAT **IS** THIS PLACE?
A FARM, OFF THE BEATEN PATH, LOTS OF LAND... OFF THE GRID, TO A CERTAIN EXTENT. WE'RE HIDING OUT HERE... WHILE WE GATHER OUR FORCES.
I DON'T KNOW IF YOU REALIZE HOW BAD IT'S GOTTEN OUT THERE, BUT IT'S NOT SAFE FOR OUR KIND.

JENNIFER TOLD ME A LOT.
SHE TAUGHT ME SO MUCH BEFORE...

...

HOW DID THEY...?

WE TRIED TO ESCAPE... A FEW TIMES. THE LAST TIME IT GOT REALLY... VIOLENT.
JENNIFER, SHE DIDN'T WANT TO GO BACK, SHE'D HAD ENOUGH. SHE FOUGHT HARDER AND SHE...
...WE WERE OVERWHELMED, BUT SHE WOULDN'T GIVE UP.
SHE PUSHED TOO HARD AND THEY... ***THEY PUSHED BACK.***

THEY SAID IT WAS AN ACCIDENT.
THEY BLAMED ME... THAT'S WHY THEY LEFT HER THERE... AS ***PUNISHMENT.***
NO.
IT WAS ***MY*** FAULT.

SHE TALKED ABOUT YOU A LOT. SHE SAID YOU'D COME FOR US.
SHE SHOULD HAVE WAITED... SHE COULD HAVE WAITED... I THINK SHE JUST GOT WORRIED WHEN I WAS THERE THAT THEY HAD TOO MANY OF US... THAT THEY WERE TOO CLOSE TO THE MERGE...
I SHOULD HAVE WORKED HARDER. I SHOULD HAVE COME SOONER. I LET HER DOWN...
...I FAILED HER.

WE ***BOTH*** DID.

LOOK, I CAN BE A **HUGE BITCH,** SOME DAYS ARE WORSE THAN OTHERS.
WE TALKED ABOUT IT AND YOU CAN STAY.
I'M SORRY.

...

OKAY, WELL... I'M GOING TO GO BACK INSIDE NOW, THEN... I'LL GET A ROOM READY FOR YOU. COOL?
...
GOOD TALK.

SHE GROWS ON YOU AFTER A WHILE...

ARE WE... OKAY HERE?
ARE YOU SURE IT'S SAFE?
FOR NOW... SEEMS SO. WE'RE PRETTY SECLUDED HERE AND WE'RE BEING SURE NOT TO DRAW TOO MUCH ATTENTION...
...THAT SAID, WITH KYLE AND ME HERE... ALONG WITH KYLE'S DAUGHTER AMBER AND NOW YOU... OUR LIGHT IS SHINING BRIGHTER AND BRIGHTER.
SO THERE WILL SOON COME A TIME WHEN OUR LIGHT SHINES TOO BRIGHT TO HIDE IT...

SO WE'RE GOING TO HAVE TO MAKE SURE THAT WHEN THAT TIME COMES IT SHINES SO BRIGHT THEY FEAR IT.
THAT'LL BE NICE.
YES, IT WILL...

THE PEOPLE OUT THERE... BACK IN ROME, THEY'RE **SCARED.**
SOME OF THEM HAVEN'T SEEN WHAT I'VE SEEN... BUT THEY CAN **FEEL** IT... THE GOOD AMONG US, THE GOD-FEARING...
...WE KNOW SOMETHING IS GOING ON.

THAT'S THE HOLY SPIRIT... IT SPEAKS TO YOU.
IF YOU'RE WILLING TO **LISTEN,** THE LORD WILL ALWAYS SHOW YOU THE WAY.
THERE'S A POWER INSIDE US ALL, PLACED THERE BY GOD.
WE JUST NEED TO NOT IGNORE IT, IS ALL.
KLIK

THEY NEED HELP, REVEREND. THEY NEED SOMEONE TO SHOW THEM THE WAY--TO HELP THEM TO NOT IGNORE THESE WARNINGS.
THE PEOPLE OF ROME... THEY STILL NEED YOU.

...

WHO ARE THEY?
THEY WORKED WITH YOUR POP-POP. THEY... DON'T STARE, TOMMY.

THIS IS NOT GOOD.
NO, NO IT IS NOT. WHAT ARE YOU GOING TO DO ABOUT IT?
ME? SURELY YOU CAN'T EXPECT ME TO--
TRY NOT TO TRIP OVER EACH OTHER WHILE TRYING TO SEE WHO CAN ACT MORE COWARDLY.

ROWLAND?
WE WEREN'T TOLD THEY WERE SENDING *YOU.*
MY ARRIVAL IS NOT OFTEN TAKEN AS **GOOD NEWS.** WHY GIVE YOU TIME TO PREPARE?
FORGIVE US.
WE HADN'T REALIZED HOW BAD THINGS HAD GOTTEN.

GET UP, YOU FOOLS.
YOU DRAW FAR TOO MUCH ATTENTION.
I SEE WHY I AM NEEDED HERE.

GO.
GO TO YOUR HOMES. AWAIT MY ORDERS. DO NOTHING UNTIL I HAVE TOLD YOU WHAT TO DO.

I WAS SCARED OF THIS PLACE AT FIRST, TOO.
NOW I KNOW IT'S PRETTY MUCH THE BEST HOME *EVER.*
IT'S BEEN A LONG TIME SINCE I'VE HAD A HOME.
YOU MAKE ME FEEL FUNNY.
WHEN I'M CLOSE, MY BODY FEELS *STRONGER* AND LESS *SLEEPY.* IT'S NEAT.
I LIKE IT.
YOU'RE KYLE'S DAUGHTER, RIGHT? YOU'RE-- YOU'RE ONE OF *US.*
WE MAKE EACH OTHER STRONGER, DID YOUR DAD TELL YOU? YOU CAN HELP US *FIGHT* THEM.

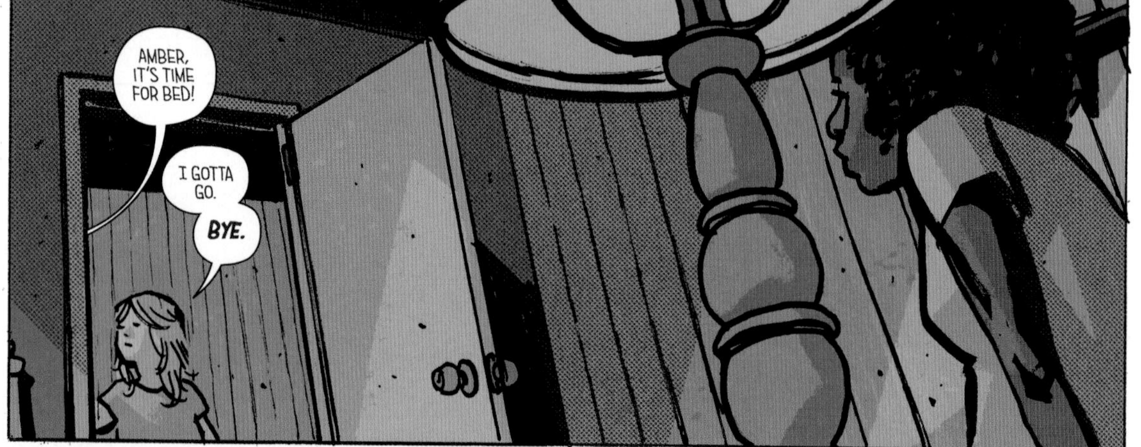
AMBER, IT'S TIME FOR BED!
I GOTTA GO.
BYE.

AMBER'S IN BED. WE'LL SEE IF SHE STAYS THERE.
YOU READY TO--
YOU SHAVED.
FINALLY.
OH, COME ON--IT WASN'T THAT BAD... WAS IT?
NO, I'D ALMOST GOTTEN USED TO IT. THE BEARD, THE BROODING... ALL THE HARD WORK WITH SIMON.
WHAT'S GOT YOU FEELING SO... OPTIMISTIC?

I DON'T KNOW... I... I CAN FEEL US GETTING STRONGER. IT FEELS LIKE EVERYTHING SIMON HAS ME DOING... IS WORKING.
I FEEL LIKE THIS WILL BE OVER SOON. WHATEVER LIES AHEAD OF US...
...I FEEL READY FOR IT.

PUT THEM IN WITH THE OTHERS.

I KNOW, HONEY. I'M SORRY.
I'M JUST CHECKING IN ON A FEW THINGS AND THEN I'LL BE HOME. JUST MAKE SURE YOU'RE DONE PACKING BEFORE I ARRIVE.
I KNOW. **BAD JOKE.** NOT FUNNY. **HELLO?**

THEY'LL GET THE BEST OF CARE HERE.
YOU KNOW THAT.

DON'T GIVE A **FUCK** HOW YOU TREAT THEM. JUST KEEP THEM OUT OF SIGHT, AND IF ANYONE COMES LOOKING FOR THEM... **YOU TELL ME.**
THINGS WILL BE **DIFFERENT** NOW.
LESS **SLOPPY.**
RN

SARAH BARNES...

YOU DIDN'T THINK I'D COME HERE WITHOUT STOPPING BY TO VISIT AN **OLD FRIEND...**
...**DID YOU?**

LOOK AT YOU.

LOOK AT WHAT YOU'VE **BECOME.**

YOU'VE ONLY GOT *YOURSELF* TO BLAME!

WRAKK

THINGS COULD HAVE BEEN SO *DIFFERENT* FOR YOU. YOU COULD HAVE HELD A SEAT ON THE COUNCIL.
WE COULD BE *EQUALS.*
DO YOU HAVE ANY IDEA HOW *VALUABLE* YOU WOULD HAVE BEEN TO US? MOTHER TO AN OUTCAST?

YOU WERE SUPPOSED TO BRING HIM TO OUR SIDE. HE WAS SUPPOSED TO BE LOYAL TO YOU.
BUT YOU JUST COULDN'T LET IT HAPPEN.

I SEE YOU... YOU LIE THERE A VICTIM, WALLOWING IN YOUR SELF-PITY. YOU CANNOT HIDE YOURSELF FROM US, THOUGH.
WE KNOW YOU, SARAH BARNES.
WE HAVE HEARD YOUR THOUGHTS. WE KNOW THE DEPTHS OF YOUR HATRED.
YOU DESPISED YOUR BOY... HATED HIM FOR BEING LEFT WITH YOU... YOU HATED THE BURDEN HE BECAME. YOU BEGGED FOR US TO EASE YOUR BURDEN... AT FIRST.
IT WAS YOUR REGRET... YOUR DEFIANCE... THAT LED TO THIS STATE YOU'RE IN. IT GREW INTO THIS... ADVERSARY YOU'VE MADE OF YOUR SON.
YOU DISGUST ME.

WRAMM

IN THE END... WHEN THIS IS ALL OVER... YOU'LL **BEG** ME TO END YOUR LIFE.
AND I'LL **MAKE** YOU BEAR WITNESS TO THE **DESTRUCTION** YOU HAVE CAUSED BEFORE I SQUEEZE THE LIFE FROM YOUR BROKEN BODY.

TO BE CONTINUED

"We're the light to their darkness.